This Book Belongs to

· · · · · · · · · · · · · · · ·

# OXFORD
## UNIVERSITY PRESS

Great Clarendon Street, Oxford OX2 6DP

Oxford University Press is a department of the University of Oxford.
It furthers the University's objective of excellence in research, scholarship,
and education by publishing worldwide in

Oxford    New York

Auckland   Cape Town   Dar es Salaam   Hong Kong   Karachi
Kuala Lumpur   Madrid   Melbourne   Mexico City   Nairobi
New Delhi   Shanghai   Taipei   Toronto

With offices in

Argentina   Austria   Brazil   Chile   Czech Republic   France   Greece
Guatemala   Hungary   Italy   Japan   Poland   Portugal   Singapore
South Korea   Switzerland   Thailand   Turkey   Ukraine   Vietnam

Oxford is a registered trade mark of Oxford University Press
in the UK and in certain other countries

2 4 6 8 10 9 7 5 3 1

British Library Cataloguing in Publication Data
Data available

ISBN: 978-0-19-273801-1 (paperback)
ISBN: 978-0-19-273802-8 (eBook)

Printed in China

Paper used in the production of this book is a natural,
recyclable product made from wood grown in sustainable forests.

Find out more about Jonathan Emmett's books at scribblestreet.co.uk
Find out more about Elys Dolan's work at www.elysdolan.com.

For Dad—J.E.

For Chris, without whom I wouldn't
have finished this book—E.D.

TOY MAKERS

ARMOURER

'Finished!' said Max. He wound up the little clockwork
horse and watched it gallop across the workbench.
Just then Max's master, the Toymaker, returned.

# CRASH!

The horse galloped off the bench and smashed to pieces on the floor.

'You were supposed to be painting puppets,' shouted the Toymaker. 'I've told you, cogs and springs are for clocks—not toys!'

TESTING
IN
PROGRESS

The Toymaker was so angry that Max lost his job.
So he went to look for a new one on the town noticeboard.

There was only one job advert and it had been there for months. It said:

BRAVE KNIGHT WANTED TO RID THE KINGDOM OF FLAMETHROTTLE THE FEROCIOUS, MAN-EATING DRAGON!

There are no other jobs, thought Max,
so I suppose I should give it a try.

Max knew that a knight should have a suit of
armour. So he went to the armourer's workshop.

'You don't look like a knight,' said Lizzie,
the girl who was working there.
'What do you want armour for?'

ARMOURER

ARMOUR
BY
SMITH

and
Daughter

TAILOR

'I'm going to get
rid of the dragon,' said Max.
  Lizzie laughed.
'You? You'll never do it . . .

'The only thing that
could get rid of that dragon is
a bigger, scarier dragon.'

But Lizzie's words had given
Max an idea. 'I think I know how
to do it,' he said, 'but I'm going to
need your help, and lots of metal!'

Later that night, Max and Lizzie crept to the entrance of Flamethrottle's cave and quietly collected the huge heap of weapons and armour, which was all that was left of the brave knights who'd dared to go inside.

Back at the workshop, they took everything to bits and began to make something new.

They worked for seven days and seven nights . . .

heating and hammering . . .

painting and patching . . .

and piecing together, until . . .

'It's **finished!**' said Max, fastening the last plate in place.

'It had better work,' yawned Lizzie.

'Of course, it will work,' said Max. 'Just as soon as we've wound it up.'

Flamethrottle awoke the next morning, opened his
terrible jaws wide and let out a deafening yawn.
'Time for breakfast!' he said. 'But no more
knights. I'm fed up with eating tinned
food. I'll pop into town and pick up a
plump princess or two.'

Licking his lips in anticipation,
Flamethrottle left the cave
to find . . .

REWARD

20,000,

APRIL

a bigger,
fiercer-looking
dragon waiting outside.

'WHAT
ARE
YOU
DOING
HERE?'
it roared.

'Er . . . I live here,'
said Flamethrottle nervously.

'NOT ANYMORE
YOU DON'T,'
bellowed the new dragon.
'OUT!'

'R-r-right,' stuttered Flamethrottle, glancing
back at his treasure. 'P-p-perhaps I could just
collect a few . . . '

'OUT NOW!'
roared the other dragon,
chasing the terrified Flamethrottle
away from the cave.

'I told you this would work!' grinned Max, as he pulled on the controls of the clockwork dragon.

'It's not over yet,' said Lizzie, as they crashed out of a forest and leapt over a startled cow.

They had almost chased Flamethrottle right out of the kingdom,
when the huge mechanical legs slowed down and then
ground to a halt.

Max fiddled frantically with the controls,
but nothing happened.
'The clockwork motor must have run down,' he groaned.

Realising that he was no longer being chased, Flamethrottle
crept back to investigate. 'What's wrong?' he asked
from a safe distance.

'Er, nothing, I'm just having a rest,' said Max, speaking through the
pipe that made the clockwork dragon's voice.
'What do we do?' whispered Lizzie. 'If he breathes fire on us,
we'll be baked alive!'
'If only we could wind up the motor,' said Max.

Meanwhile, Flamethrottle had crept
closer to get a better look at the
other dragon.

'What's that big key for?'
he asked.

Then Max had another of his ideas. 'PLEASE don't touch that!' he called. 'It's very important.'

'What did you tell him that for?' hissed Lizzie.

'Why is the key important?' demanded Flamethrottle.

'Because I'm a mechanical dragon,' replied Max. 'If you turn it my legs will lock and I won't be able to chase you.'

'Really?' said Flamethrottle, gleefully. And he grabbed the key and gave it a turn.

'Please don't turn it again,' wailed Max. 'If you do, my claws will lock and I won't be able to grab you.'

'Ooh,' said Flamethrottle. And he couldn't resist giving the key another couple of turns.

'Please, stop!' whimpered Max once more. 'Or my jaws will lock and I won't be able to eat you.'

So, of course, Flamethrottle seized the key and turned it again and again until it would turn no more. . .

'Now I've got you,' yelled Flamethrottle triumphantly.

'No, now I've got you!' said Max, pulling hard on the controls.

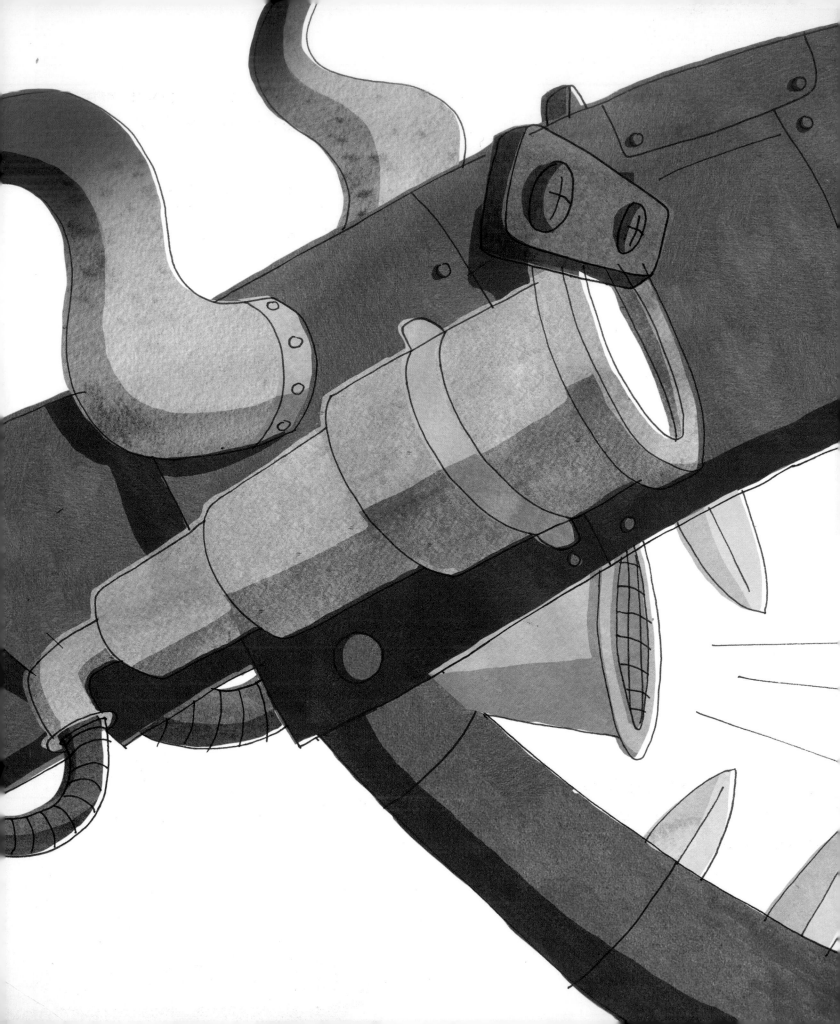

The fully wound clockwork dragon sprang forwards with gaping jaws.

# 'YAAYGHHH!'

screamed Flamethrottle, as the razor-sharp teeth came snapping towards him.

And—without stopping to see if the metal dragon's legs and claws were also working—he scrambled off, out of the kingdom, and was never seen again.

Everyone was so
pleased to be rid of
Flamethrottle that Max
and Lizzie were given
the dragon's treasure as a
reward. They used it to set
up a clockwork toyshop.
   The shop sold everything
from clockwork archers to
clockwork zebras, but their
most popular toy was—well,
can you guess?

Yes, it was their little
clockwork dragons,
of course!